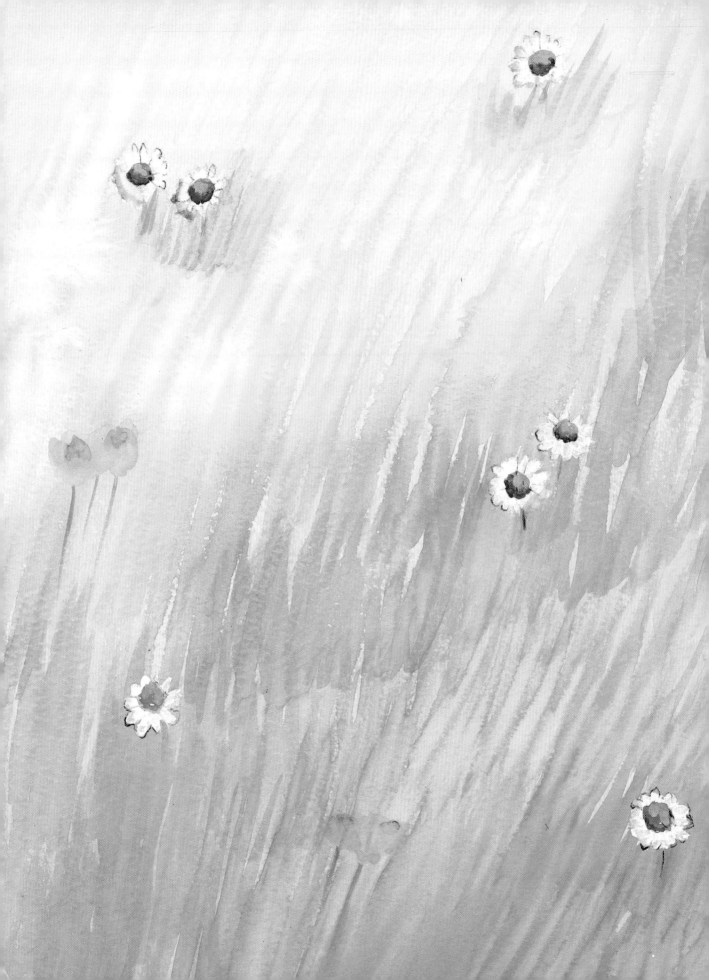

for Robert

Designed by Louise Millar

Printed and bound in Belgium by Proost
for the publishers Piccadilly Press Ltd.,
5 Castle Road, London NW1 8PR

ISBN: 1 85340 617 1 paperback
1 85340 612 0 hardback

3 5 7 9 10 8 6 4

Set in 32pt Bembo

A catalogue record for this book is available from the British Library

Also available in this series:

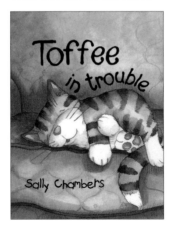

TOFFEE IN TROUBLE
ISBN: 1 85340 594 9 (p/b)
1 85340 589 2 (h/b)

*Sally Chambers lives in Hayes, Kent. She has written and illustrated a number of
picture books. Piccadilly Press also publish BARTY'S SCARF and
BARTY'S KETCHUP CATASTROPHE, about an independent-thinking sheep.*

Toffee takes a Nap

Sally Chambers

Piccadilly Press • London

It's a lovely sunny day.
Perfect for Toffee
to take a nap.

Toffee starts to dream.

Then she rolls over . . .

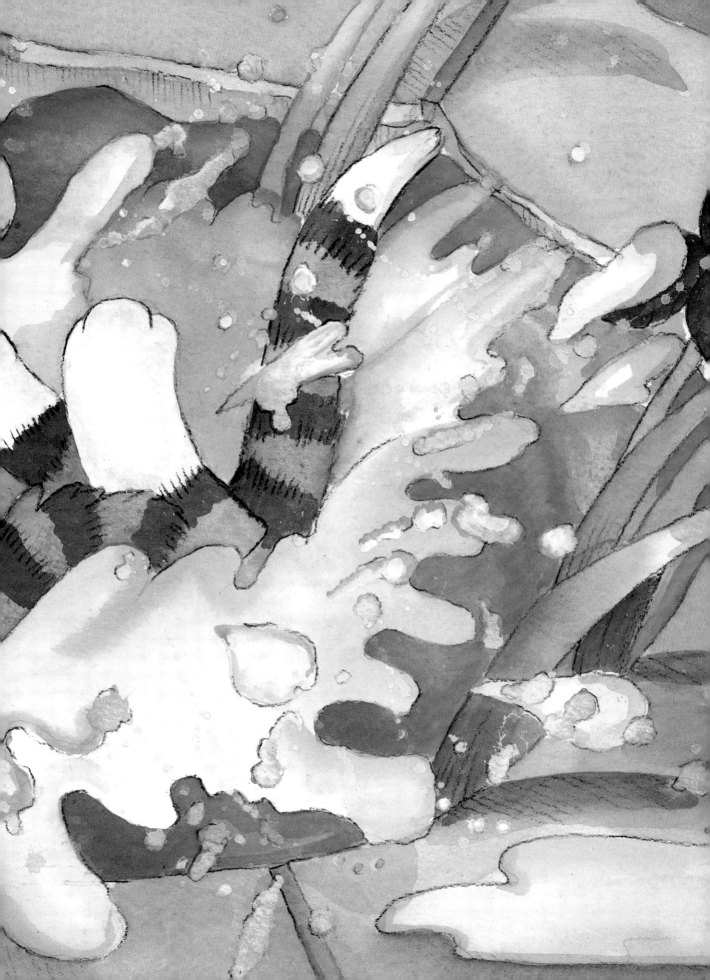

Oh dear! Poor Toffee!

What a terrible surprise!

Toffee dries off in the warm sun.

She tries to go back to sleep.

Tweet! Chirp! Tweet!
The birds are too noisy.

The shed is a quiet place.

But Tom thinks it is his shed.

What is Toffee
to do . . . ?

hiss, growl, hiss

Toffee doesn't want
to fight.

She is frightened.

She runs inside.

Toffee is very tired.

Where can she sleep?

Not here.

Not here.

Toffee knows . . .

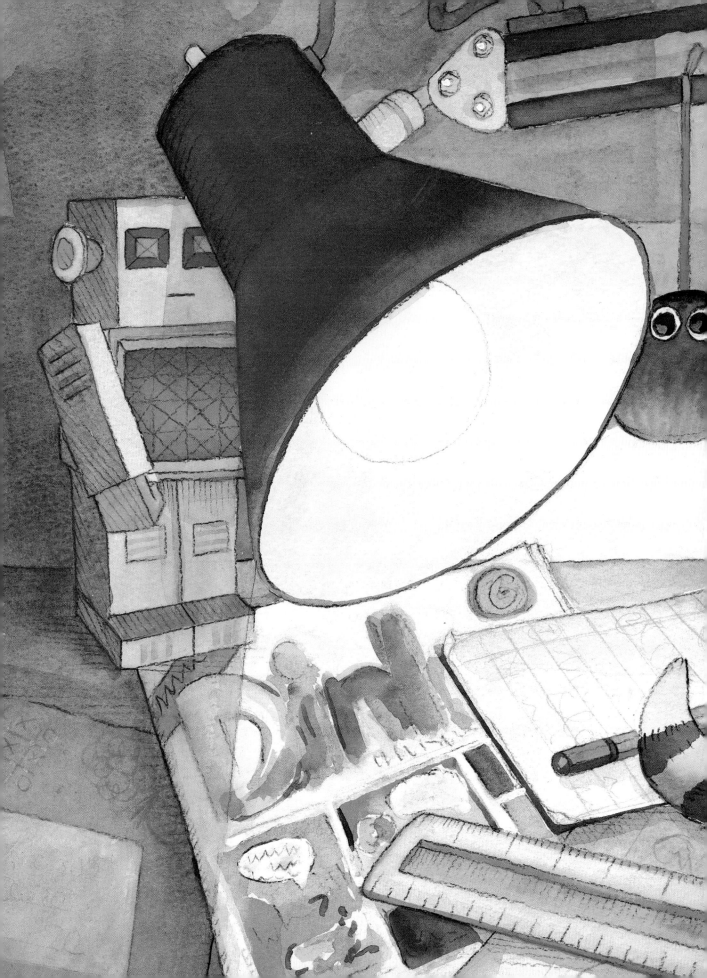

Night-night, Toffee.

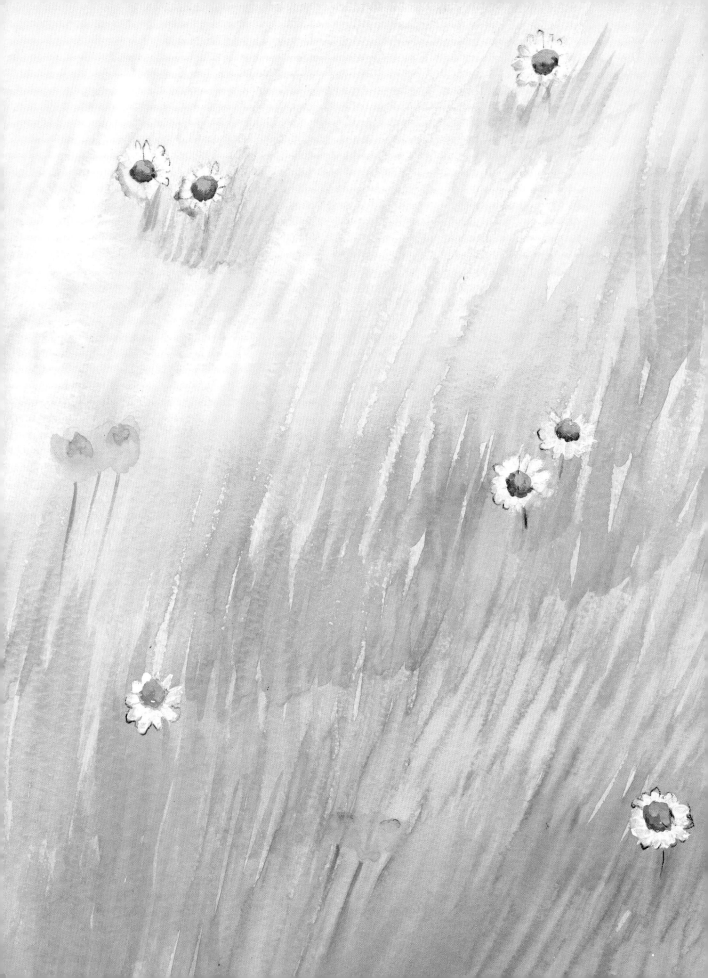